The Secret Puppy

Holly Webb

Illustrated by Sophy Williams

stripes

For Zoe

For more information about Holly Webb visit:
www.holly-webb.com

STRIPES PUBLISHING
An imprint of Little Tiger Press
1 The Coda Centre, 189 Munster Road,
London SW6 6AW

A paperback original
First published in Great Britain in 2012

Text copyright © Holly Webb, 2012
Illustrations copyright © Sophy Williams, 2012

ISBN: 978-1-84715-233-6

A CIP catalogue record for this book is available
from the British Library.

Printed and bound in the UK.

10 9 8 7 6 5 4 3 2 1

Chapter One

Daisy jumped out of the car, looking eagerly round the field. It was the first time she'd been camping, and she was really excited.

"Is this our tent?" she asked her dad, gazing at the big green and red tent they'd parked next to. "It's huge!"

Dad nodded. "It can sleep six, the lady on the phone said. So that means you and Oliver can each have a room to sleep in."

"A pod," Oliver corrected him. "They're called pods, Dad."

Daisy rolled her eyes. Just because Oliver had been camping with Cubs, he thought he knew everything. He always thought he was cleverer than Daisy anyway, being a year older than her. Oliver had enjoyed Cub camp so much he'd begged and begged for them to go camping in their summer holidays. But Daisy didn't mind. Usually they rented a cottage by the seaside, and it was nice to do something different. Riverside Farm had loads of things to do, and lots of animals to make friends with. Mum wasn't quite so convinced about tents, though.

She'd finally agreed to camping, but she'd insisted that they went to the kind of campsite where the owners would put up one of their tents for you, if you wanted. Even though Oliver said that was cheating.

"Pods, sorry, Mr Camping Expert." Dad lugged one of the big boxes out of the car. They might not have needed to bring their own tent, but there was still loads of stuff. They'd hired a little gas stove and some cooking things from the campsite as well, but they'd had to bring sleeping bags and mats – and folding garden chairs to sit on. Dad had said he couldn't cope with sitting on the ground for a fortnight. Then there was all the food and clothes. Mum had insisted on bringing raincoats and wellies, just in case.

"Can we go and explore?" Daisy asked hopefully. "Look at the river! It runs right by our tent!" She'd known there was a river running through the campsite – the name was a bit of a giveaway – but she hadn't realized they would be camping so close to it. She could imagine curling up to sleep in their tent, hearing the water rushing along. "There's a bridge to get to the rest of the farm. Oh, and look! Ducks! There might even be baby ones. And I have to go and see the horses!"

"I want to go and look at the pool," Oliver put in. "We won't be long, Mum."

Mum shook her head. "Not just yet. You can explore soon, I promise. We need to unpack, then Dad and I will come with you to have a look round. I need to know where you're going to be before I let you disappear off."

Oliver looked like he was about to argue, but then he sighed and grabbed an armful of sleeping bags out of the car.

"Can I have this room?" he asked, unzipping one of the doors off the main living area. The three bedrooms stuck out at the sides and the back of the tent, and there was a sort of open canopy at the front, which they could cook under if it was raining.

"I thought it was called a pod?" Daisy said sweetly, dodging the sleeping bag he flung at her. "If you're having that one, can I have this one at the back?"

Dad nodded. "I don't see why not. They're all the same size."

"And that leaves us the furthest away from Oliver and his snoring," Mum pointed out.

Daisy picked up the sleeping bag Oliver had thrown at her (it was hers) and unzipped the door to the back bedroom. It was actually quite big, she realized, feeling surprised. She'd expected the tent to be tiny, but her bedroom even had a back door! She unzipped it and peeked out, smiling to herself as she saw the river running along a few metres behind the tent. She wasn't going to tell Oliver she had her own secret door – he'd only want to swap.

Luckily, it didn't take too long to unpack – Daisy didn't have to put her clothes away, since there wasn't anywhere to put them. She spread out her sleeping bag and mat, thinking that she was actually looking forward to going to bed. She'd never slept next to a river before.

"Daisy? Are you ready? Shall we go and have a look round?" her mum called. Daisy jumped up, stepped out of the pod and zipped the door closed behind her.

"Will you be all right, sleeping in there by yourself?" her mum asked a little anxiously, but Daisy beamed at her.

"It's lovely! Why wouldn't I be all right? It's only like having my own room at home, Mum."

Her mum nodded. "I suppose we're very close to you, if you do get nervous."

Daisy giggled. "I could probably reach a hand out of my bedroom door and tickle your feet if I stretched."

"So what shall we go and see first?"

Dad asked. "There's a little café that sells ice creams. Do we fancy that?"

"Ice cream?" Oliver poked his head out of his pod. Daisy nodded eagerly. It was very warm in the tent; an ice cream sounded perfect.

Mum looked at the little map she'd picked up when they'd arrived at the campsite. "Once we've done that, and we've had a quick look around, I don't mind if you two go off on your own, as long as you promise to tell us where you're going and be back when we say."

Daisy smiled. She didn't usually get to go to places on her own, although Oliver sometimes walked to school with his friends now he was in Year Five. Being at the campsite was like a big adventure.

They walked past lots of other tents on the way to the café, which was part of the old farm buildings. They'd all been converted now, with a little food shop, and a gift shop, and a craft area that did workshops they could sign up for. Daisy really fancied having a go at the jewellery one.

There were quite a few other boys around – including a couple about Oliver's age playing football outside a tent close to theirs. But Daisy couldn't see many girls, apart from a few little ones. Still, she didn't mind. There was loads of stuff to do, and she was looking forward to exploring on her own.

"No one's brought dogs with them," she said to Dad, as they walked along the line of tents. Daisy loved dogs, and she'd thought that there might be a few staying in tents with their owners.

"I don't think dogs are allowed, are they?" Dad said. "I'm sure I read that somewhere on the website. They might frighten the animals, I suppose."

Daisy sighed, and Dad put an arm round her shoulders. "Never mind, Daisy. There's lots of other animals here. Don't forget those piglets, and the shire horses."

Daisy nodded. She *was* excited about the piglets, but a dog to play with would have been even nicer. She'd been trying to persuade her parents that they should get a dog for ages, but it didn't seem to be working. Mum was worried that their garden wasn't big enough, although Daisy was sure that people with much smaller gardens than theirs had dogs. Besides, there was a huge park close to their house, so it didn't really matter. But Mum said that wasn't the same.

She'd tried to get Oliver to help her persuade them, but he wasn't really bothered. He already had a pet, a red-legged tarantula called Otto that he'd got for his ninth birthday. Daisy hated spiders. If Oliver wanted to upset her, he'd open his bedroom door and pretend he was letting Otto out of his tank. It made Daisy scream. That was one of the good things about camping – Otto couldn't come too. Oliver had left him with his friend Max to look after.

Daisy shuddered, just thinking about the enormous spider. How could Mum and Dad let Oliver have such a horrible pet? And Otto was huge. Not that much smaller than a very small dog, really...

"Come on, slowcoach!" Oliver turned to look back at Daisy, as she started to trail behind the rest of the family. "Don't you want your ice cream?"

Chapter Two

"Someone *has* brought a dog; I'm sure I heard it barking as we walked across the yard!" Daisy pulled at her dad's sleeve. "Well, just little dog noises, really – more like whining than barking."

The teenage girl scooping out the ice creams smiled at her. "That's the puppies you can hear. They're in the stable on the other side of the yard."

"Puppies?" Daisy asked hopefully.

"Uh-huh. German shepherds. My mum breeds them – we've got so much space with all the old farm buildings, the dogs have their own special room. It's the one with the sign over the door that says Riverside German Shepherds."

"Are we allowed to see them?" Daisy said. She loved German shepherds, they were so noble-looking.

"Maybe – you'll have to ask my mum, Julie. You'll have met her in reception, I bet."

Daisy nodded. The lady who'd given them the map and told them where their tent was – she'd definitely been called Julie. And she did look quite like Amy, the girl in the café, with dark, curly hair. "I'll ask," she told Amy.

"Thanks!" Daisy wasn't usually all that good at asking for things – she was too shy. But for the chance to meet some puppies, she could be brave enough to talk to someone she didn't know.

Once she'd eaten her ice cream, Daisy persuaded Mum to return to reception with her, while Dad and Oliver went to look at the climbing wall.

"Hello! Is everything all right? Do you like your tent?" Julie asked them, smiling.

Mum nodded. "It's lovely. Much bigger than we'd expected." She gave Daisy an encouraging look.

"Would it be OK…" Daisy gabbled. "I mean – please could I see the puppies? Amy said there were puppies."

Julie laughed. "There are. Six of them, they're ten weeks old now. Do you like dogs?"

"Yes. I'd love to have my own dog. Do you have lots?"

"Usually only Lucy, she's the puppies' mum, and Sally, that's her sister. We don't breed very many puppies – just two litters a year. And then we either sell them to be pets, or sometimes they go to be working dogs. Quite a lot of our puppies are police dogs now."

Daisy nodded. She knew that German shepherds made good police dogs because they could be trained so well. They were used as sniffer dogs, and search and rescue dogs, too.

"Don't they get a bit too big to be pets?" Daisy's mum asked doubtfully.

Julie shook her head, laughing. "No! Well, they are big, I suppose. We have Lucy and Sally in the house with us, when they aren't having pups and living in the puppy room, and they do take up a lot of the kitchen in their baskets. But to be honest, it's all down to how well-behaved a dog is. If you train a big dog properly, it takes up less room than a small dog!"

It sounded silly, but Daisy knew what Julie meant. Her friend Millie had a miniature dachshund, who was gorgeous but also totally spoilt. Millie's whole family ran around after her. She definitely took up a *lot* of room…

"I was actually going over to check on the pups in a minute anyway," Julie said, glancing at her watch. "You can come with me if you like?"

"Yes, please!" Daisy said eagerly. "Do they need feeding? Puppies need lots of meals, don't they?"

Julie looked at her in surprise. "I didn't think you had a dog?"

Daisy smiled shyly. "Oh, I don't. But I love reading about them. I got a brilliant book all about dogs for Christmas. I've read it four times, and it says lots of stuff about puppies. Are your puppies nearly ready to go to new homes, if they're ten weeks old?"

"Yes, their new owners are coming to visit this week and next." Julie came out from behind the reception desk, and led Daisy and her mum back up the path towards the main yard. "We've been lucky, we've got a name for ourselves for breeding good-natured dogs. There was a feature in the local paper about training police dogs, which had a gorgeous photo of two of our puppies with their police handlers. After that, lots of people wanted a Riverside puppy. All the puppies in this litter will go to people on the waiting list."

"Oh…" Daisy gave a tiny sigh. She had been daydreaming that Mum would fall in love with one of the German shepherd puppies, and she'd finally be able to persuade her to get a dog. She was pretty sure Dad was already coming round to the idea. He had admitted he quite fancied the early morning walks to get some fresh air before he started work. He and mum worked together from home, designing websites, and he spent most of his time stuck in front of the computer. Daisy sighed again. There was no point even thinking about it. A dog would be the best thing to take home from a holiday ever, but if the puppies were all reserved, it was no use.

They'd reached the main yard now, and Julie opened the door to the puppy room. "We converted it specially, you see, so that they've got an outdoor run as well. Now it's so hot we've been able to leave the door to the run open all the time, so they can get some fresh air. And we take them out into our garden too."

Just inside the room was a wire pen with a gate in it, and stretched out on a fleecy blanket was a beautiful German shepherd. She looked exactly like the photos from Daisy's book, with golden brown legs and ears, and a black face and back. She had huge dark eyes, and she was staring thoughtfully at Daisy. She didn't look fierce – just watchful.

And Daisy could understand why.

Tumbling around her were four beautiful puppies, and she was making sure that Daisy and her mum were safe to be around them. The puppies, however, weren't worried at all. They bounced over to the edge of the pen and scrabbled excitedly at the wire. If they stood on their hind paws, they could almost put their noses over the top. Two more puppies dashed in from the outside run and flung themselves at the wire too, yapping excitedly.

Daisy's mum laughed. "Oh my goodness. I can see why you have them out here rather than in the house…"

"We do bring them into the house too, to get them used to being around people and to being careful with the furniture," Julie explained. "But not usually all at once. It's a big old farmhouse, but eight German shepherds are a bit much for any home."

"They're gorgeous," Daisy breathed. She'd been expecting the puppies to be cute, and they were, but it still wasn't quite the right word for them. Although they were really soft and fluffy, they didn't have round little puppy faces. They already had lovely long German shepherd muzzles, and upstanding ears. They weren't just cute – they were *handsome*.

Then one of the puppies put his head on one side, and gazed at Daisy. His ears twitched and wriggled. Daisy laughed, and crouched down to get a better look.

"Oh, he's got a flop-over ear," she said, wishing she could stroke it. The puppy was the darkest of the litter, with lovely browny-gold fur, and black markings on his face, like a sort of curly T-shape that went over his eyes and down his nose.

Julie crouched down next to her. "Lovely, isn't he? Their ears start to straighten up around now; he's just taking a bit longer than the others. Sometimes they're about five months old before their ears stand up properly."

The puppy seemed to know that they

were talking about him. His brothers and sisters had lost interest in Daisy, and gone off to chase each other around the pen and tussle with the toys that were scattered about. But he stayed by the wire, watching her intently with his dark, intelligent eyes.

"What's his name?" she asked Julie.

"Well, we try not to name them, even though it's difficult sometimes. It's nice if their new owners can choose their own names," Julie explained.

"He looks really clever," Daisy said.

"He *is* sweet," Mum agreed.

Daisy looked up at her eagerly, and Mum shook her head. "Don't get too excited! We couldn't have a big dog like that."

"But – we might be able to get a dog? Another kind of dog?" Daisy whispered.

"We're thinking about it," her mum admitted. "Dad would really like a dog, and I had a dog when I was your age. She was called Cola, because she was exactly cola-coloured. You and Oliver are old enough to be sensible with a dog now. So maybe we can have a think about it when we get home…"

"Oh, Mum!" Daisy flung her arms round her mum's neck.

The puppy by the wire looked up at them, wondering what was going on. His floppy ear straightened up for a second, and then flopped over again. The girl looked down at him, and he licked her hand through the wire and made her laugh. He liked her.

Daisy crouched down by the wire again. "I might be able to have a puppy like you," she whispered.

"You can stroke him, if you're gentle," Julie told her, and Daisy slowly stretched out her fingers, so as not to scare the puppy, and rubbed his golden fur. She sighed contentedly.

Julie was smiling. "If you want, Daisy, you might be able to help me with socializing the puppies – getting them used to different people before they go to their new homes."

"Can I, Mum?" Daisy asked hopefully. She had two weeks at Riverside Farm. It was the perfect opportunity to show Mum and Dad what a fantastic dog-owner she would be. She was scratching the puppy behind his velvety ears now, and he was leaning blissfully against the side of the pen.

Mum nodded. "Just don't get too used to German shepherds, Daisy! I know they're gorgeous, but if we do get a dog, it'll definitely be something smaller."

Chapter Three

The flop-eared puppy galloped across the grass, and skidded to a halt before he landed in the rose bushes – he knew they were prickly. Then he turned round and galloped the whole way back again. All the puppies loved playing out in the garden. Now they were getting bigger they spent loads of time running around. Julie had given them an old football, and his two sisters were scrapping over it in the middle of the lawn. He thought about going to join in, but then he spotted a blackbird landing on top of the old brick wall.

The puppy stalked over, his tail wagging from side to side. He hoped that the bird would come down, so he could get a better look. The blackbird stared back, its head on one side, but it showed no sign of coming any closer. The puppy crept towards the bird, and then made a mad little dash up to the wall, jumping and scrabbling at the bricks and barking hopefully. The blackbird fluttered its wings in fright, squawked and flew away.

"I think you have to sneak up on them a bit more to catch them,"

Daisy said behind him. At the sound of her voice, the puppy forgot about the blackbird, and raced over to her, his tail wagging madly. He  planted his fat front paws on her knees, and did his best to lick her face all over.

"Hello there!" Daisy smiled. They were nearly a week through their holiday, and she had visited the puppies every day so far. Oliver had been off doing canoeing and raft-building on the river, but although Daisy had gone to a couple of the craft sessions, she by far preferred playing with the puppies.

Daisy's dad had come to find her the day before, and he'd apologized to Julie for Daisy hanging around the puppy pen all the time.

"Not at all – it's great to have someone else to play with the puppies," Julie had explained. "Most of them are going to family homes, so they need to get used to being around children. Daisy's helping me out! And the puppies love her. She's very patient."

Daisy glowed when Julie said that. She really wanted Mum and Dad to think of her as someone who was good with dogs – someone who could be helpful if *they* got a dog. But most of all she was pleased that Julie thought the puppies liked her. Especially her favourite puppy, the one with the flop-over ear. When no one was listening, Daisy had secretly named him Barney. It seemed to suit him – it sounded cheeky and matched the clever glint in his eyes. She did play with the other puppies too, but Barney always came over to her and if she sat down in the pen, he would snuggle up with his nose on her lap. He'd even fallen asleep like that a couple of times.

Lucy, the puppies' mother, wasn't in the pen with them today. She still spent a lot of time with the puppies, but as they were completely weaned from her milk and eating puppy food she liked a bit of time off now and then. Julie said that all she did when she wasn't with the puppies was flake out in her basket, next to her sister Sally, looking exhausted.

Occasionally she'd get up to have a big drink of water. Daisy thought she must be grateful to do this without three or four puppies coming to see what she was doing and then joining in and splashing her.

That morning, Daisy and Oliver had gone for a walk with Dad down to the nearest village, as they both had some holiday money to spend. Oliver had bought a water pistol, and Daisy had spent some of her money on a pack of puppy treats. It was bulging in her shorts' pocket now. She'd asked Julie if it was OK to give them to the puppies, and she had said it was fine, as long as it was only a few at a time.

Just then, Julie came up to the door of the pen. "I was thinking, Daisy, if you like, you could take one of the puppies out for a little walk round the yard for me," she suggested. "I need them to get used to seeing lots of people, and walking on a lead too. They'll all be going to obedience classes as soon as they get to their new homes, and it'll be good if the lead isn't a complete surprise."

Daisy nodded. That would be amazing – like having her very own dog! "Which puppy do you want me to take?" she asked, hoping it would be Barney.

"You can choose, as long as I know who've you've taken – that way I can make sure they all get a turn. Don't take them out of the yard, though, and only walk them for a few minutes. They need to start small and build up."

Daisy glanced at Barney. She was sure he would love the yard. He was such a curious little dog. Maybe people would think he belonged to her, she thought. He could be her secret puppy, just for a short while.

Julie gave her a collar and a lead to put on Barney, and showed her how to fasten it so that it would stay on, without being too tight.

Barney wriggled and whined with excitement as Daisy tried to put the collar on him. He wasn't really sure what was happening, but it was definitely new and different. And Daisy was there. He loved it when she came to play with him. She would spend ages rolling a ball back and forth for him to chase, or stroking his ears.

Eventually Daisy managed to get the lead on him, and she led Barney out of the pen, and then out of the door on to the yard, with the puppy waltzing joyfully around her feet. "Careful, Barney!" Daisy laughed. "You're going to trip me up." She glanced round to check that Julie wasn't listening. She didn't want her to know that she'd named the puppy – he wasn't hers to name, after all.

"We're going on our first walk!"

Barney stared at the people in the farmyard, eating ice creams from the shop, visiting the piglets in their stall, or stroking the two shire horses. Children were running around, laughing and shouting.  He'd never seen so many people at once. He was used to Julie and the occasional visitor, but that was all. He stopped frisking about and twitched his tail in a nervous sort of wag.

Daisy crouched down next to him. "It's OK, Barney. I know it's a bit scary. Let's just go round the edge of the yard a bit..." She coaxed him along, being careful not to pull on the lead, until they reached a bench. She sat down, snuggling Barney up against her knees. She wished she could pick him up and have him on her lap, but Julie had told her that the puppies weren't allowed on the furniture when they went in the farmhouse, because they were going to be just too big when they were older. So she thought it was probably best if he didn't go on benches either. But she could still cuddle him. *And* give him a reward, she suddenly remembered!

Daisy pulled the foil pack of treats out of her pocket and tore it open, shaking a few into her hand. "Here, Barney!" She held them out to him.

Barney sniffed the delicious treats and glanced round. He'd been staring worriedly at the horse that was leaning its head out of its stall and watching him. It was enormous! But the treats smelled so good, he soon forgot to worry. He crunched them happily, and Daisy giggled as his soft, whiskery nose nuzzled against her hand, followed by a wet, velvety tongue – Barney was making sure he hadn't missed any crumbs.

Daisy sat there enjoying the sunshine, and the admiring glances from the people passing by. She knew she ought to take Barney back and give one of the other puppies a turn, like Julie had said. But not just yet…

"Daisy!"

Daisy jumped. She hadn't noticed her mum standing beside the bench. She smiled. "Hi, Mum! I didn't see you."

"I was coming to check if you wanted to go to the craft session this afternoon – they're making friendship bracelets. I thought you might like to take some home for Millie and Eva."

"OK." Daisy nodded. "That sounds fun. Thanks." She looked sideways at her mum, feeling slightly worried. Why was she frowning like that?

"Daisy, this is the same puppy again, isn't it?" Her mum sat down next to her, and gently rubbed Barney's flop-over ear. He panted happily, enjoying the attention.

"The same as what…?" Daisy said, stalling. She was pretty sure she knew what her mum meant, but she didn't know why it mattered.

"The one with the floppy ear – the one you're always playing with."

"Yes… But Julie asked me to take him out and show him the yard. It's to get him used to being on a lead."

"And did she say you could give him the treats too?" Mum asked her.

"Yes! You know I wouldn't feed him anything without asking!" Daisy protested.

"Mmm. But I don't think Julie would've meant you should give treats just to this puppy. Have you taken any of the others out like this?"

"No, but…" Daisy trailed off.

"Daisy, if you fall in love with this puppy, what's it going to be like when we go home? We've got less than a week here now, sweetheart. I don't want you to be sad when you have to leave him." Mum sighed. "And actually, it's not very fair on him either."

Daisy looked up in surprise. "What do you mean? Barney really likes me! He looks forward to seeing me, I know he does!"

"Exactly. Dogs get very attached to people, Daisy. Next Saturday he'll be waiting for you to come and see him, and you'll be on your way home!"

Daisy's eyes filled with tears. She'd known she was really going to miss Barney, but she'd been trying not to think about it. He was her holiday dog – her secret, special puppy, just for these few days.

But she hadn't thought about how *he* was going to feel when she'd gone.

"You've even named him, haven't you?" her mum said. "You called him

Barney just then. Julie said she tried not to name the puppies."

"I didn't mean to…" Daisy said quietly.

"I think you need to stop spending so much time with him," her mum told her gently. "He'll be going to his new owners soon. He needs to love them, Daisy. Not you."

Daisy nodded slowly. Mum was right. She'd have to play with all the puppies, not just Barney, so that he didn't think he was her special one… Daisy sniffed. She couldn't do it, she knew she couldn't. He *was* special!

She'd just have to stop seeing the puppies altogether.

She stood up, and Barney followed her, his ears twitching anxiously.

Something was wrong. Daisy's voice had changed, and her eyes looked all shiny. He whimpered, and Daisy patted him, but not the way she usually did. It was almost as though she didn't want to touch him any more. Barney laid his ears back, and looked up at her worriedly. But Daisy wasn't looking at him.

"I'll take him back," she whispered. "Sorry, Barney…"

Chapter Four

Barney sat by the wire front of the pen, watching the door out to the yard. The top half of the stable door was open, and two of his brothers were dozing in a patch of warm sun, while the others played. But Barney didn't want to leave his watch to join in. It was hard to tell when someone was going to open the door, because there were footsteps going past all the time, people wandering across the yard to the café and the craft workshops. But he was listening anyway, waiting for Daisy to come back.

She hadn't been to see him for ages, and he didn't understand why. Until a couple of days ago, she'd come to the puppy pen every day to cuddle him, or play games with all the puppies. But specially with him. She really loved him, he could tell from the way she looked at him.

It had all changed after they'd gone out for their walk in the yard. He didn't know what had happened, but everything had gone wrong.

Barney slumped down by the fence, resting his head on his paws and watching the other puppies tumbling about, chasing after a rope toy. Suddenly, his ears twitched. There was a scuffling noise at the door. Was someone coming? Perhaps it was Daisy!

The door opened, and Barney sprang up, jumping at the wire and scrabbling at it with his paws.

It wasn't Daisy after all – just Julie, with a man and a boy he hadn't seen before. "Oh, that one's excited!" the man said. As soon as he saw them, Barney dropped down, and stood gazing sadly out through the wire.

"He's a very sweet puppy, very friendly," Julie said, smiling. But as she opened the pen, Barney slunk away into the corner, leaving his brothers and sisters to be fussed over by the visitors.

"I think I saw his picture on the website!" The little boy pointed to Barney. "He's the one with the floppy ear. Please can we have him?"

"Is he all right?" the dad asked, as his son crouched down to look at Barney. "He doesn't look very friendly. Don't get too close, Davey."

Julie was frowning. "He's usually very affectionate," she murmured.

"Can I stroke him?" asked Davey.

Julie smiled. "Of course you can."

But when Davey tried to stroke Barney, the puppy wriggled further into the corner of the pen.

"I don't think he likes me," Davey said sadly. Just then, one of Barney's sisters rubbed her head against his knees, making him laugh. "But this puppy's nice, Dad!" He sat down on the floor to make a fuss of her, and she climbed into his lap, licking his hands excitedly.

His dad laughed. "I think she's chosen you, Davey." He glanced over at Barney. "I hope the other puppy's OK."

Julie smiled. "I'm sure he's just having an off-day," she said. But she couldn't help feeling surprised. This little one was usually so friendly –

maybe he was missing Daisy? Daisy's mum had explained that she thought Daisy was getting too attached to the puppies and it would be better if she didn't spend so much time with them. Julie had agreed – but she hadn't realized that this puppy had already bonded with Daisy, too.

Daisy's mum did all she could to cheer her up, but she wasn't having much success. Everything seemed to remind Daisy of Barney. She wouldn't go back to see the puppies at all. She said it made her too sad. Her mum almost wished she hadn't said anything, but then the end of the holiday would have been heart-breaking if she'd let Daisy go on falling in love with Barney.

"I've booked a treat for you today," Mum told her, as she passed her the box of cornflakes on Wednesday morning. They were just about used to eating in folding camp chairs by now – it was a weird juggling act, trying to pour cereal and milk, and not tip the bowl into your lap. Dad said that if they came camping again, they'd need a folding table, too.

Daisy was pretty sure she *didn't* want to come again. Even to a different campsite. It would remind her too much of Barney. Still, she was trying not to be a misery, and ruin the holiday for Mum and Dad and Oliver. "What is it?" she asked, making herself sound interested.

"Pony trekking!" Mum said, smiling. "I saw a leaflet in reception."

"I don't want to go horse-riding, Mum." Oliver looked up from his cereal. "I said I'd go and play football with Liam and Tom."

Mum frowned. "Which ones are Liam and Tom?"

"Mu-um!" Oliver sighed. "They're in the red tent at the other end of our row."

"Well, that's good because I didn't book the riding for you anyway."

Mum grinned at him. "I didn't think it was your sort of thing. Daisy and I are going together."

Daisy smiled at her. She knew how hard Mum was trying to make her happy. She did love horses, and she'd wanted to try riding for ages.

"Actually, we should finish up breakfast quickly," Mum said, checking her watch. "We're booked in for ten."

The stables were about ten minutes' drive from the campsite. Somehow, Daisy felt a bit better once they'd driven out of the Riverside gate. She was still really missing Barney – especially as she kept wondering if he was missing her too. But she could squash the sadness down inside her, and be just a little bit excited about going to the stables.

The pony trekking was brilliant. Daisy's pony was a grey called Billy, who was very well-behaved. He also seemed to know the paths they were trekking down, so Daisy didn't feel as if she had to worry about where they were going. Mum's chestnut pony, Cracker, was a bit more of a handful. She kept trying to stop and eat mouthfuls of grass, which made Mum slide forwards. At one point Mum had had to hang on round Cracker's neck to stop herself falling into a prickly-looking hedge!

Carly, the riding instructor, kept telling Mum to pull Cracker's reins so that he would leave the grass alone. By the time they got back to the stables, Mum told Daisy that she thought she might have pulled her arms out of their sockets!

They helped to untack the ponies and rub them down, and they were just saying goodbye when Daisy gasped.

"What's the matter?" Mum asked.

Daisy didn't say anything. She was staring at a beautiful German shepherd, who was standing at the door to one of the stalls. A dark bay horse was leaning out, and it looked as if they were talking to each other.

"That's Frankie," Carly said. "He's our stable dog. Isn't he gorgeous?

He goes on the rides sometimes too. He really loves Pepper, the bay horse over there. If Pepper's out, he follows along." She smiled at Daisy and her mum. "Actually, you're staying at Riverside, aren't you? That's where he came from."

Daisy tried to smile. "Really?" she whispered. Frankie was probably related to Barney somehow. "Can we go now?" she muttered to Mum.

Mum hugged her. "Course we can. Oh, Daisy. I'm really sorry…"

All the fun of the pony trek was swallowed up by how much Daisy was missing Barney.

She was never going to see what he looked like when he was all grown up, like Frankie. She brushed her arm across her eyes to rub away her tears. Why was she being so stupid? She'd known all along they'd never be able to take Barney home. Mum and Dad hadn't even said for definite that they could get a dog, just that they were going to talk about it. And Barney almost belonged to someone else anyway. But seeing gorgeous Frankie had made it all seem so much worse.

At least they only had two more days at the campsite. This was the worst holiday ever, Daisy thought miserably as she trudged back to the car. And only a few days ago, she'd thought it couldn't get any better.

Chapter Five

By the next day, Barney was sick of waiting by the front of the pen. Why had Daisy stopped coming to see him? What if there was something wrong? He prowled around the run all day, sniffing the edges of the pen and trying to find a way out. He needed to go and find Daisy. He was sure she was still somewhere close.

Barney hardly ate any of the meals that Julie gave him. As usual, she brought the puppies their last meal of the day through from the farmhouse at about nine. As she put the bowls down in the pen, Barney didn't race over like the others. He just went on sniffing carefully at the wire.

Julie shook her head and looked at him worriedly. "I really hope you cheer up a bit before tomorrow," she said, kneeling down next to the puppy to stroke him. "Your new owner's coming to see you. She called me today, to tell me she's chosen you from those photos I emailed her. She's been waiting for the perfect puppy for a while, she said, and she thinks you're the one. She wants to take you to dog shows."

Barney nuzzled her hand gently. He might be miserable, but he still liked Julie. He thumped his tail on the scruffy grass of the pen.

"Good boy," Julie said. "Are you missing Daisy? Her mum said she was getting too fond of you, and she was worried it was going to make it hard for her to say goodbye." She sighed. "I probably shouldn't have let her come to see you so much, but she was having such a nice time... Oh dear, I think that's what it is, isn't it?" She rubbed his ears. "Don't worry. You'll have a lovely new owner soon."

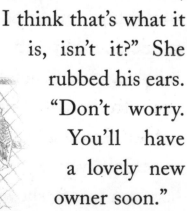

As she stood up, Barney sighed and lay down by the wire of the pen, looking out at the garden. Julie frowned. He really *was* missing Daisy. And she was sure Daisy would really be missing him, too.

Julie walked out of the gate, latching it carefully behind her. As she headed back to the farmhouse, she wondered if there was anything she could do to help the puppy.

She didn't notice Barney's ears twitching curiously. One of them pricked right up, and the other followed suit but then flopped over again the way it always did.

He'd found a hole in the wire fence.

Daisy lay on her tummy at the edge of the river, watching the ducks. Oliver had gone off to play football again, and Mum and Dad had gone to do the washing-up after dinner. Daisy thought Mum was probably still feeling sorry for her, after she'd been so upset at the stables. She'd suggested that Daisy read a book in the tent, or find some friends to chat to. But Daisy had spent so much time playing with the puppies, she hadn't really made friends round the campsite like Oliver had.

It was starting to get dark, and the ducks swam slowly away. Dinner had been late – the gas stove had taken ages to boil the water for the pasta – so it would be time to go to bed soon.

She wriggled up on to her elbows and flicked a little stick into the water, watching it float away downstream. Maybe she could play pooh-sticks with herself… But then she decided that was just boring. And a bit sad.

She'd go and read in a minute, she thought, dabbling her fingers in the water and wishing the ducks would come back.

Barney scrabbled at the little dip in the packed earth under the wire fence. The run backed on to the path up to the camping area. If he could just get underneath, he was sure he could find Daisy.

The other puppies were still eating, and his mum was over at the farmhouse, so no one noticed him  scraping, and digging. Finally, he wriggled underneath the wire, and out on to the path.

He trotted away, sniffing the long grass and wondering which way to go. He could hear people talking – their voices carrying through the quiet evening, as children were called back into the tents, and their parents settled down to chat for a while before going to bed.

He sniffed again carefully. He couldn't smell Daisy yet, but perhaps she would be where he could hear all those voices. He hurried down the path, his tail wagging a little, head down, searching. He could smell the river, although he wasn't sure what it was. It smelled different and exciting, full of the scents of mice and water rats. Then he spotted some ducks, swimming slowly along the far bank, and went faster, eager to get a closer look.

It was as he was hurrying over the little bridge that he caught Daisy's scent. He stopped dead, sniffing the air and looking around hopefully.

She was there! Lying by the water, as though she were waiting for him! He was so desperate to see Daisy that going the whole way to the end of the bridge seemed too slow. With a joyful bark, Barney jumped through the railings, landing just on the bank, his back paws scrabbling in the damp mud at the water's edge. Kicking up the mud, he raced along the grassy river bank, and threw himself at Daisy, who stared at him in amazement.

"Barney! It's you!" Daisy hugged him, laughing. She'd heard the bark, and the mad scuffling and splashing, but she'd never thought it would be Barney coming to find her. "How did you get here? I wonder if Julie's looking for you – did you sneak out somehow?"

Barney laid his head on her lap, and sighed contentedly. She wasn't cross. Whatever had happened to make her stop coming, she still loved him. He could tell from her voice.

"Oh Barney, I've really missed you." Daisy ran her hand gently through the thick fur on his back. "I think you've got bigger, and it's only three days since I last saw you."

Barney wasn't sure what she was saying, but he liked listening to her.

He wriggled himself closer, so that his paws and shoulders were on her lap too. He wasn't going to let her disappear again.

Daisy frowned. "I'm not supposed to be around you. Mum says." She swallowed, feeling a lump rising in her throat. "And she's probably right. She thought it was just going to make both of us miserable. I'm going home soon, you see…"

She knew she ought to take Barney straight back to the farmhouse and tell Julie he'd got out somehow. But she couldn't. Not just yet. She wanted to cuddle him a little bit longer. Only till Mum and Dad came back from doing the washing-up…

But then they might say it was time

for bed, and Dad would take Barney back instead. Daisy shook her head suddenly. She knew she couldn't let that happen. Mum was right – she was just making it harder for herself, but she didn't care. Being away from Barney hadn't stopped her missing him. It didn't look like he'd forgotten about her, either; he'd obviously come to find her. Would another day of being around him really make it any worse for them both?

Daisy gathered Barney into her arms and stood up. "You're so heavy," she whispered to him lovingly, and Barney licked her ear. He liked being carried. "Come on. Mum and Dad will be back soon. And Oliver. We're going to have to be a bit sneaky."

For just one night she could pretend that Barney was *her* dog... Daisy carried him round to the back of their tent, to her own secret door, and put him down beside her while she unzipped it. Then she crawled inside, beckoning Barney after her. He pattered in happily, sniffing around the funny little room, before slumping down on her sleeping bag.

"Good idea," Daisy muttered. "I'll tell Mum and Dad I'm tired. Are you hungry, Barney?" she whispered, remembering the nearly full pack of dog treats that was still in her pocket.

She hadn't been able to throw it away. "Julie said she usually gives you supper at about nine. Did she leave the gate open afterwards?" Daisy frowned. She couldn't imagine Julie doing that. She was so careful. "I know I ought to take you back, but I can't. Not yet. I'll take you first thing tomorrow."

She fed Barney a handful of treats, and watched him gulping them down while she put on her pyjamas, and slipped into her sleeping bag.

Barney sniffed thoughtfully round the walls of the tent, and then lay down next to Daisy, staring up at her, his dark eyes glinting in the dim evening light.

Daisy rubbed his head and Barney wriggled, his ears twitching. Then Daisy heard what he'd heard – voices.

Mum and Dad were on their way back. They mustn't see him!

Quickly, she arranged her fleece blanket half over her sleeping bag and half over Barney, so he looked like some of her stuff. In this light, when Mum looked in to check on Daisy, she'd never be able to tell he was a dog.

"Sssh…" she whispered, feeding him another treat. "You're my secret, OK?"

Barney snuffled up the treat, and then snuggled closer to her. He didn't mind being quiet, as long as he was with Daisy.

Chapter Six

Daisy woke up early, blinking in the soft sunlight that was coming through the side of the tent. She felt deliciously warm and very happy, but she couldn't quite think why.

Then Barney wriggled and yawned next to her, and she remembered.

"Are you awake, Daisy?" her mum called. "You went to sleep really early last night, are you feeling OK?"

"I'm fine," Daisy called back, twitching the blanket over Barney, in case her mum decided to look in and check on her. "Can I go for a walk before breakfast, Mum?"

"I suppose so..." Mum sounded surprised.

"We're going home tomorrow," Daisy added. "I just want to make sure I – um – see everything..."

"You're mad," Oliver muttered from deep inside his sleeping bag. He hated getting up in the morning.

"I'll be back soon," Daisy promised, flinging on some clothes and unzipping her secret door. Barney stuck his nose out as soon as she'd opened the zip enough, sniffing happily at the damp grass.

"Come on," Daisy whispered. "Julie gets up early to feed you lot. She'll probably have noticed you're missing by now."

She hurried over the bridge, with Barney pattering after her, his little shiny black claws clicking on the wood.

"Ugh, it's cold." Daisy shivered, wishing she'd looked at the weather before she'd put on her denim shorts. At least she'd brought a hoodie. "I think it might rain," she added sadly. "On our last proper day." She swallowed. Her last day at Riverside. After tomorrow, she wouldn't be able to see Barney again.

For a moment, she was tempted to run back to the tent and try to hide him, somehow smuggle him into the car and take him home. But she knew it would never work. It was just a silly daydream.

"Barney!" she called, hurrying down the path. She wanted to get this over with.

Barney trotted behind her, his head hanging a little. He could tell where they were going. He didn't want to return to the pen with his brothers and sisters. He'd liked being with Daisy much more.

Daisy had decided she'd better take Barney to the front door of the farmhouse, as the door in the yard would be still be locked. She wasn't quite sure what she was going to say – just that she'd found the puppy. Which was true, even if it wasn't the whole truth. She slowed down as she came up the path, suddenly worrying that Julie might ask her difficult questions.

Barney hung back at the gate and whined, wishing he was still in the tent. He wanted to snuggle up next to Daisy and have some more of those treats. There was a strong wind blowing, and he didn't like the feel of it whistling round his ears at all.

Daisy came over and picked him up gently. "I know," she muttered in his ear.

"I don't want to leave you, either. But you're not mine, Barney." She sniffed and knocked on the front door.

It flew open almost at once, and Julie was there with a phone in her hand.

"Oh! He's here, it's all right! Yes, Daisy's got him! I'll call you again in a minute." She ended the call, and hugged Daisy and Barney. "That was Amy, she'd gone to look along the road for me; we were worried he might have got out there. Oh, Daisy, you star, where did you find him?"

"Um, he found me," Daisy told her. "By the river."

"Thank you so much. I went in to feed the puppies this morning, and realized he was gone. He'd dug a little hole under the wire of the run; I don't know how he squeezed himself out." She patted Barney gently. "I really thought we might have lost you. I'm going to have to block up that hole, aren't I?" She looked Barney over anxiously. "He's all right? He wasn't limping or anything?"

Daisy shook her head. "He looks fine to me."

"His new owner's coming to see him today, which just made it all worse – can you imagine having to explain that we'd lost him!" Julie sighed. "At least, I hope she'll be his new owner. I've not actually met her yet, but she sounds very keen."

Daisy nodded, and tried to blink away the tears that had suddenly filled her eyes. "Is she going to take him today?" she managed to ask.

Julie put an arm round her. "No. She just wants to meet him. I'm sure she'll be nice, Daisy. He'll have a lovely home. And you'll get a dog of your own soon. I told your mum and dad how helpful you were, and how you'd be a brilliant dog owner."

"Thanks," Daisy said quietly. But it wasn't the same. She wanted Barney, and she knew she couldn't have him. Blinking away her tears, she passed the fat furry bundle to Julie, and Barney whimpered, wriggling back towards her.

"I'd better go. I just went for a walk before breakfast. Mum doesn't know where I am."

"Come and see us later," Julie suggested. "I want to give you something to say thank you."

Daisy nodded, and hurried off up the path.

Barney stared after her, whining miserably. He'd gone and found Daisy, and she'd been pleased to see him. Why was she leaving him again?

"That's really nice of Julie," Mum said, when Daisy explained about going over to the farmhouse later. "You just found Barney wandering along by the river?"

"Yes." Daisy nodded. She had. She just hadn't been very clear about *when*, that was all. "And so I took him back."

Mum eyed her thoughtfully, and Daisy tried not to go red as she ate her cereal. She was pretty sure that Mum thought there was more going on than she was telling.

"I'm supposed to be going canoeing on the river this morning," Oliver said dismally, staring out from under the canopy at the dark grey sky. As Daisy walked back from the farmhouse, it had started to rain.

Dad shrugged. "Well, you're going to get wet anyway..."

Oliver made a face. "I know. It just doesn't feel like holiday weather any more, that's all."

"Maybe it'll blow over," Mum said. But it didn't look like it would.

Daisy walked down to the canoe shed with Oliver and Dad later that morning, while Mum nipped to the village shops. Daisy was going to go over to the farmhouse once she'd watched Oliver for a little while. It was nice of Julie to want to give her something, but it was making her feel a bit guilty.

It took ages for the canoeing to get started. Oliver had to be kitted out with waterproofs and paddle, and told all the safety rules. The instructor kept suggesting that Daisy join in, too. In the end, she told Dad she was going to the farmhouse, just to get away before she was forced into a canoe.

When she went back up to the farmhouse, Julie was already talking to someone – and Daisy gulped, remembering what she had said.

It was Barney's new owner.

Daisy didn't really like the look of her. That might be because she was jealous, Daisy thought, trying to be fair. But it seemed strange that the woman was in a smart dress, when she was coming to see a litter of muddy-pawed puppies.

Her frilly umbrella kept trying to turn inside out, too. Daisy hung around by the gate, trying not to get in the way, but now it seemed the woman was leaving.

Julie folded her arms and watched as the woman went down the path. She looked a bit annoyed. Daisy wondered whether Julie had discovered that Barney had stayed in her tent all night. But Julie smiled when she saw her.

"Was that Bar— I mean, the puppy's new owner?" Daisy asked her, in a small voice.

Julie shook her head. "No. It should have been. But she's decided she doesn't want him after all."

"Why not?" Daisy stared at her. How could anybody not want him?

"Because of his floppy ear. She's looking for a show dog, you see. It would disqualify him in the show ring."

"But you said he'd grow out of it." Daisy frowned.

"Yes, he probably will. But he's the only one of the litter whose ears haven't straightened up, and she thinks it won't. So – she doesn't want him."

Daisy's eyes widened, as thoughts swirled around her head. "But … does that mean he's still for sale?" she stammered, looking up at Julie in sudden hope.

"Well, yes – there's no one else on the waiting list at the moment, so he is, I suppose. Oh! Daisy, come back, I've got some sweets for you!"

But Daisy was gone, racing back along the path to the river, to tell her dad they had to give Barney a home.

Chapter Seven

"Dad! Dad! You have to come!" Daisy dashed up to where her dad was huddled in his waterproof, watching Oliver, who was out on the river now.

"What's the matter?" Dad looked worried, but Daisy laughed.

"Nothing! Nothing's the matter, it's a good thing! Barney's new owner doesn't want him. We can buy him!

We could take him home with us tomorrow! You have to come and talk to Julie."

"What? Slow down, Daisy, I don't understand." Dad was frowning, and for the first time since Julie had told her the news, Daisy stopped to think. She'd been so excited that Barney was for sale again that she hadn't even considered whether her parents would say yes.

"Barney... The German shepherd puppy – the one I really like. I had to stop going to see him because he was going to belong to someone else, and it wasn't fair on him. But he isn't anyone's now, Dad!"

"What are you two talking about that's so important?"

Daisy jumped. Mum had come up behind her without her even noticing.

"Daisy says that the puppy…" Dad began. He sounded worried.

"It's Barney, Mum." Daisy's words were tumbling over each other as she tried to explain. "The lady who was supposed to buy him changed her mind. So we can have him – can't we? You said you were seriously thinking about getting a dog. Please, please can it be *this* dog?"

"But Daisy, a great big German shepherd?" Her mum sighed. "I know he's cute and little and fluffy now, but think how big Lucy and Sally are! We couldn't have a dog like that."

"Why not?" Daisy swallowed hard. She couldn't cry now. She needed to persuade them, and they'd never listen if she was crying.

"Well, our garden isn't big enough. The house isn't big enough either, come to that! Imagine a huge dog in our living room, Daisy. He'd take up the whole sofa."

"He wouldn't be allowed on the sofa, Mum. We'd train him properly, like Julie said. So he wouldn't make a mess and stuff. He wouldn't be like Millie's dog." Daisy dug her nails into the palms of her hands, forcing herself to sound calm and sensible. "There's a dog-training class that meets in the same hall as Brownies, I've seen a poster. And we're so close to the park. I'm nearly old enough to take him there on my own."

Her mum shook her head. "I'm not sure about that."

"Well, OK, with Oliver then. And I *will* be old enough soon." She turned to her dad. "You said you wanted to go for walks with a dog, Dad!"

Dad sighed. "I do, Daisy. This is all just a bit sudden. And your mum's right. We never thought of having such a big dog. German shepherds need loads of exercise, and they're bred to be working dogs. I'm not sure they're great pets."

"But you don't know Barney," Daisy pleaded. "Not like I do. He'd be a wonderful pet." She was losing, she could tell. Mum and Dad didn't understand, they weren't listening. Tears started to stream down her face.

"Don't cry, Daisy." Mum went to put an arm round her, but Daisy pulled away and ran off back to the tent.

How could this be happening?

Barney could be hers, after all, but she was going to lose him.

Barney prowled up and down the run, the fur on the back of his neck prickling. He hated being back in his pen, even though he'd been pleased to see the other puppies again. He wanted to be back up at the campsite with Daisy.

Especially now. It was still raining heavily, and the wind was rising too. He didn't like the feel of it. It was really howling through the pen, and whistling round the yard too, rattling all the doors and making the puppies jump and whimper.

He needed to go back to Daisy, and make sure she was all right. But Julie had carefully blocked up the hole under the wire fence, digging a board in so he couldn't get out that way again.

He was stuck.

"You'll just have to share Otto with me instead," Oliver said, grinning. "I'll let you feed him, if you like. Spiders don't need walking all the time."

He was smirking at her over his bowl of soup, and suddenly Daisy couldn't stand it any longer. They'd been stuck in the tent in the pouring rain for ages, and Oliver was driving her mad. She'd tried being calm and persuasive and sensible, and everyone had treated her like a silly little girl who didn't know what she was talking about.

Right. So she would be a silly little girl. It didn't matter, anyway. Mum and Dad had refused to listen to any more discussion about Barney. Mum had said that no meant no, as though Daisy was about three. She had even gone to see Julie, and explained that much as they'd love a dog, they just couldn't have one as big and demanding as a German shepherd.

"I hate you and your stupid spider!"
Daisy screamed. She flung herself at
Oliver, not even noticing that she'd
spilt the tomato soup all down his
front. His folding chair tipped over and
they both fell to the ground.

"Daisy, stop it!" Mum yelled, and Dad pulled her off Oliver, looking furious.

"Look at the state of you both!" he snapped. "You'd better go to bed, Daisy. And you too!" he added, as Oliver sniggered. "You were teasing her. I'm going to be really glad to get out of this tent and get home tomorrow."

Daisy zipped herself into her pod, changed out of her tomatoey hoodie and shorts, and crawled into her sleeping bag. She buried her face in the fleecy blanket she'd used to cover up Barney. It still smelled of him. She couldn't stop crying now. She hated it that Oliver and Mum and Dad could hear her. Maybe the drumming of the rain on the tent and the howling of the wind would hide the crying a little.

Barney was so close. That was the awful thing. Just across the river and down the path. He would be curling up to go to sleep with the other puppies now. She could almost see him…

But they were going home tomorrow, and then she'd never see him again.

Barney shook his ears worriedly. Julie had closed the door out to the run when she'd come to bring the puppies' supper, as it was raining so hard. But he could still hear it hammering on the roof, and the wind battering around the yard. All the puppies hated the eerie noises.

But he was the only one left awake now. The others had settled into an uneasy sleep, huddled together for comfort. Barney sat down by the wire fence of the pen and whined miserably. Something was wrong, he was sure of it. All this wind and rain. More than ever, Barney wanted to be with Daisy. He was scared and she would make him feel better, but that wasn't the real reason he wanted to be with her. He was scared for *her*. The wind had been blowing round the tent even that morning, and he hadn't liked the way it shook and juddered about. He needed to be there to guard her and keep her safe.

He jumped in fright as a particularly strong gust of wind whistled round the yard and blew the door of the puppy room off its latch. The bottom of the door creaked open, clattering against the wall. It was usually locked at night, but the horrible weather had meant that Julie was racing about, distracted, and she'd forgotten to lock it when she brought the puppies' food over from the farmhouse.

The other puppies wriggled and whimpered in their sleep, but none of them woke up. Barney shivered as the cold wind cut through the room, but then his ears pricked up – or one of them did, anyway.

The door was open now! He could go and find Daisy!

If he could get out of the wire pen...

He scratched at it uselessly, but he only hurt his paws. And it was no good trying to dig under it, as he'd done outside. This was a solid floor. He would have to go over the top of the wire.

Barney stood on his hind paws, reaching up as far as he could. To his surprise, he was actually as tall as the fence now. His front paws hung over the top, and he could get his head over it, just. He kicked and scrabbled at the floor, trying to push himself up, but he wasn't quite tall enough. Then his claws caught on the bar across the top, and he kicked harder – he was climbing! He scrabbled again, getting the other back paw up, and heaved himself over the edge of the pen, teetering on the top for a few seconds. Then, almost without realizing how he'd done it, Barney was on the floor – on the other side of the wire.

He looked nervously at the door. It was still banging to and fro, and it was dark and wet outside. For a moment he wished that he was back inside with his brothers and sisters, where it was warm and safe.

Then he shook himself. He needed to find Daisy. He marched across the floor, and nudged the swinging door hard with his nose.

Out in the yard the rain was

hammering down so hard he could barely see. Barney shrank back against the wall, trying to think how to get to Daisy. When he'd found her before, he'd gone out of the side of the run instead, straight on to the path.

Ears laid back against the driving rain, Barney set out across the yard to where he thought he remembered the entrance was, his tail tucked between his legs. He'd never seen anything like this before. It had been a hot summer – so hot that all the ground was dry, and as he reached the path there were huge puddles where the water couldn't soak in fast enough. Barney hurried round them, shivering as the rain soaked through his thick fur. He was fairly sure he knew where he was going now, but as he came closer to the river his ears laid back even further than before.

It hadn't looked like this yesterday.

The hot weather had left it low and sluggish, but now the torrential rain had filled the river up again, so that it was racing along, sticks and debris jostling about in the dark water. It was starting to overflow its banks, too.

Barney hesitated at the end of the bridge. Water was lapping around his paws, but he knew that to get to Daisy, he had to go across. The river just seemed so much bigger and scarier now than it had before. It stretched out beyond the bridge on the other side too, and that was what made Barney move at last.

On the other side of the bridge was Daisy's tent – and the water had almost reached it.

Chapter Eight

Barney raced across the bridge, splashing through the water at the end, which was halfway up his legs. The ground sloped up from the river to the tents, but only a little. Snatches of moonlight shone on the dark water that was rising slowly but surely towards Daisy's pod.

He reached the tent and barked as loud as he could, right outside Daisy's secret door. He hated this water – it was black and scary, and he didn't want it anywhere near Daisy.

Inside the tent, Daisy whimpered and turned over in her sleep as she heard Barney. The barking just merged into her dreams, making them even more terribly real. Barney was racing along behind the car as they drove away, barking and barking. He didn't understand why she wasn't taking him with her.

Neither did Daisy.

He was out of sight now. Although Daisy was still staring out of the car window, she couldn't see him at all. So why could she still hear him barking?

Daisy sat up suddenly, clutching her sleeping bag around her. That wasn't

part of her dream! That was actually
Barney! He'd come to find her again.
Smiling, she unzipped her back door.

"Barney, ssshhh! You'll wake up
Mum and Dad – oh, wow!" Daisy
gasped as she saw the flood water rising
up towards the tent.

Barney whined crossly. Why was she still sitting there? She needed to get out, and the others too! He darted into her tent pod and grabbed her sleeve in his teeth, pulling her.

"Barney, you came to rescue us!" Daisy whispered, staring at him in amazement. "How did you know? OK, OK." She reached out to unzip her front door, the one that led into the living area. "Mum! Dad! Oliver! The river's flooding, we have to get out of the tent!"

"What?" There was a scuffling noise, then the zip opened and Dad's head appeared round the door.

"It really is! Barney came to tell us, Dad, he's outside. He barked to wake me up!"

Dad dashed across the living area into Daisy's pod, and stared out silently for a moment. Then he turned round and dashed back, grabbing his wellies. "I don't how that dog knew, or how he got here, but it's lucky he did. Your mum's just getting dressed. The water will be in the tent any minute. Oliver, up, now! We need to get out of the tent!"

"Where are we going?" Daisy asked, pattering across the living area to grab her wellies and waterproof.

Dad frowned. "The farmhouse. We need to let them know the river's flooding. I'm sure they'll find somewhere for us to sleep. And help us get our stuff out too. But I'm going to go and tell the people in the tents closest first." He hurried out, pulling on his raincoat over his pyjamas as he unzipped the front of the tent.

Barney was standing in the doorway of Daisy's pod, watching anxiously. He wanted her out of there now, before that black water came any closer.

"He really came to tell you what was happening?" Oliver said, as he struggled out of his pod, still sounding sleepy.

Daisy nodded proudly. "He must have got out of the puppy room again."

"That's amazing." Oliver patted Barney, but he hardly noticed. The water was getting closer and closer. He barked warningly at Daisy, and pulled at the leg of her pyjamas with his teeth.

"He wants you to get out of here," Mum said appearing from her pod. "Get your boots on, Oliver. We'd better go."

Daisy patted her leg and stepped outside. "Come on, Barney."

It was eerie watching the water creeping up the grass towards the tents. Dad had woken up the families in all the tents nearest the water, and they were starting to come out, dressed in boots and waterproofs.

Barney stood in front of Daisy's tent, looking nervously at the water. They needed to get back across the bridge, but he hated the thought of going across the flooded bank. It would be high up his legs by now. He glanced up at Daisy, her face white in the darkness. She looked scared too. He whined and took a couple of steps towards the bridge. He had to get her to the farmhouse, where she'd be safe.

Dad came hurrying back with his torch. "Good dog. We're coming now."

Daisy could hear the other families coming along behind him, the children pointing Barney out as the dog who'd woken everyone up to rescue them.

"Is he your dog?" one of the boys that Oliver played football with asked her admiringly.

Daisy caught her breath, staring hopefully up at her dad. He nodded. "After this, I think he is," he muttered. "I don't care how big he's going to get. He's a little star."

"They're trained to be rescue dogs, aren't they?" Mum said. "I suppose you can see why. Come on. We'll work out how we're going to manage when we're in the dry."

Daisy put her hand on Barney's back. *Her* puppy's back. Dad was holding her other hand tightly, as though he didn't want to let her go.

Barney looked up at Daisy, and splashed forward into the water, head down, determined. He was going to make sure Daisy was safe, even if it meant going back across the river.

"It's almost coming over the bridge," Daisy said to Dad.

Dad nodded. "We need to tell them at the farm, fast. Then they can get round in the Land Rover over the other bridge, and make sure everyone's OK." He grinned at Daisy as they followed Barney off the bridge, through the water again to the path on the other side. "We'd better tell them we've got this little one, as well."

"And that we're keeping him?" Daisy said, hesitantly. Had Mum and Dad really meant it?

But her dad nodded. "And that we're keeping him," he agreed.

Daisy gripped the thick fur under her fingers even tighter. Barney looked up at her, his ears twitching with relief as they came out of the water at last. Holding his head up high, he set off down the path, leading them all the way to somewhere safe and dry.

"Look!" Daisy pointed further down the path – lights were coming towards them from the farmhouse, and anxious voices were calling. "It must be Julie. They're coming to get us."

Dad hugged her. "We'll have to tell her she's too late, Daisy. We've already been rescued!"

"I still can't believe the river rose that quickly." Julie shook her head. "It's never been that high. We were lucky there were only a few tents close enough to be flooded."

"Did everyone manage to get their

stuff out?" Daisy's mum asked.

Julie nodded. "It's all drying in the stables. And most people are heading home today, like you, so they only had one night squashed up in our spare rooms, and the empty holiday cottage. I don't think we'll use that end of the field for camping again, though – it could have been so much worse."

Daisy yawned, leaning against Mum's arm. She'd spent the rest of last night sleeping on Julie's living-room floor, wrapped up in spare blankets. She'd let Oliver have the sofa – she wanted Barney next to her, and she didn't want him to get into bad habits. She wasn't going to do anything that might put Mum and Dad off.

Barney didn't look tired at all.

His eyes were sparkling, and he kept twisting his head round to look at the collar and lead that Julie had given Daisy for him. She said they'd need them when they stopped to let him out on the way home.

Home! Daisy smiled to herself. She still could hardly believe it. Dad was packing the car now, carefully making a safe space in the boot for Barney. It meant Daisy and Oliver would have loads of bags round their legs, but they didn't mind.

"I think we're ready," Dad said. "Julie, do you reckon he's got enough room in here?"

Julie looked over. "He should be fine." She smiled at Daisy. "I'm so glad he's going home with you. It's perfect."

Daisy lifted Barney into the car, patting him gently as she took off his lead. "I can't believe he's really ours," she told Julie, giggling as Barney licked her cheek. "Not just for the holiday, but for ever."